SIMPLE PICTURES ARE BEST

SIMPLE PICTURES ARE BEST

story by NANCY WILLARD

pictures by TOMIE dePAOLA

A Voyager/HBJ Book
Harcourt Brace Jovanovich, Publishers
San Diego   New York   London

HBJ

FOR FLEUR

Requests for permission to make copies of any part of the
work should be mailed to: Permissions,
Harcourt Brace Jovanovich, Publishers,
Orlando, Florida 32887.

Library of Congress Cataloging in Publication Data
Willard, Nancy.
Simple pictures are best.
(A Voyager/HBJ book)
SUMMARY: A shoemaker and his wife being photographed
for their wedding anniversary keep adding items to the
picture despite the photographer's admonition
that "Simple pictures are best."
[1.   Photography—Fiction]
I.   De Paola, Thomas Anthony.   II.   Title.
[PZ7.W6553Si   1978]   [E]   78-6424

ISBN 0-15-332875-4   (Library: 10 different titles)
ISBN 0-15-332890-8   (Single title, 4 copies)
ISBN 0-15-332950-5   (Replacement single copy)

The shoemaker and his wife lived in a small house so far from other houses that their road seemed the last road in the world.

"Everything we want is here," said the shoemaker.

Behind the house they planted a garden. The sunflowers grew right up to the roof, and a Hubbard squash lolled fat and ripe as a pig.

A one-eyed cat arrived one day, caught all the mice in the house, and stayed.

During the day the shoemaker worked at his bench and made up poems.

His wife Ellen painted pictures and baked pies.

They both worked in the garden.

In the evening the shoemaker played the fiddle and his wife played the spoons while the shoemaker sang,

> "The little black bull come down the meadow,
> Hoosen Johnny, Hoosen Johnny,
> The little black bull come down the meadow
> Long time ago."

One day Ellen said, "Tomorrow is our wedding anniversary. I would like to have our picture taken."

So the shoemaker called a photographer, and the photographer arrived with a camera so large that a dozen swallows could have nested in it.

Behind the photographer walked a little boy holding a suitcase.

"James," said the photographer, "hand me my film."

So James opened the suitcase and took out a packet of film, and the photographer put the film into the camera. Then he put the camera on a tripod.

"I'm ready," said the photographer. "Where would you like the picture taken?"

"In front of the house," said the shoemaker.

"In the garden," said Ellen, "to show off our squash."

One said yes and the other said no, and so it went until James said, "Why don't you pick the squash and put the squash in the picture and take the picture in front of the house?"

So the shoemaker and his wife went into the garden and picked the squash, and together they carried it out of the garden. Then they sat down in their chairs in front of the house.

But no sooner had Ellen sat down than she jumped up again.

"If we're going to put the squash in the picture, we should put the carrots in it, too. They're much prettier than the squash."

"Simple pictures are best," said the photographer.

But Ellen had already run off to fetch the carrots.

When she returned, the photographer said, "Madam, what clothes will you be wearing for the picture?"

Now Ellen did not want to admit that she was, at that moment, wearing her best dress. So she said, "I shall wear my blue hat."

"I like your red hat better," said the shoemaker.

One said yes and the other said no, and so it went until James said, "Why doesn't Ellen wear the blue hat and the shoemaker wear the red one?"

"Simple pictures are best," warned the photographer.

But the shoemaker had already run off to fetch the hats.

When he returned, the photographer said, "Shoemaker, what shoes will you be wearing for the picture?"

Now the shoemaker did not want to admit that, though he made shoes, he never wore them.

"My old shoes," said the shoemaker.

"I like your new ones best," said Ellen.

One said yes and the other said no, and so it went until James said, "Why don't you wear the old ones on your feet and the new ones on your ears?"

"Simple pictures are best," warned the photographer.

But the shoemaker had already run off to fetch the shoes.

When he returned, he was wearing his old shoes on his feet and his new shoes on his ears and the red hat on his head, and he sat down, with the squash in his lap, next to Ellen in her blue hat, with the carrots in her lap, in front of the house.

The photographer threw a black cloth over the camera and put his head under it.

"We're ready," said Ellen. "What's wrong?"

"Madam, you have a tail under your chair," said the photographer in a muffled voice.

"Meow!" said the chair.

"Why, it's the puss cat," exclaimed Ellen, and reaching under her chair, she brought out the one-eyed cat. "If we're going to put the squash and the carrots in the picture, we must have Puss in it, too. She's much prettier than the squash and the carrots."

"Simple pictures are best," warned the photographer.

Puss sat down between the shoemaker, wearing his old shoes on his feet and his new shoes on his ears and the red hat on his head with the squash in his lap, and Ellen, in her blue hat with the carrots in her lap, in front of the house.

The photographer threw his black cloth over the camera and crawled under it again.

"We're ready," said the shoemaker. "What's wrong?"

"Shoemaker, you keep moving your hands," said the photographer in a muffled voice.

"I don't know what to do with them," said the shoemaker with a sigh. "I'm not comfortable without my fiddle."

"Well, then, get your fiddle," said James.

"Simple pictures are best," warned the photographer.

But the shoemaker had already run off to fetch his fiddle.

When he returned, holding his fiddle and wearing his old shoes on his feet and his new shoes on his ears and the red hat on his head, he sat down, with the squash in his lap, next to Ellen in her blue hat with the carrots in her lap, and the puss cat sat between them in front of the house.

The photographer threw his black cloth over the camera and crawled under it.

"We're ready," said Ellen. "What's wrong?"

"Madam, you keep moving *your* hands," said the photographer in a muffled voice.

"I don't know what to do with them," said Ellen with a sigh. "I must hold something, too. I shall hold my spoons."

"Your spoons!" exclaimed the shoemaker. "That will look odd unless you're holding a dish as well. You can hold the spoons and the blueberry pie you baked this morning."

"Simple pictures are best," warned the photographer.

But Ellen had already run off to fetch her spoons and pie.

When she returned, she sat down, in her blue hat with the carrots in her lap and her spoons in her hand and her blueberry pie in her arms, next to the shoemaker, holding his fiddle and wearing his old shoes on his feet and his new shoes on his ears and the red hat on his head with the squash in his lap, and the puss cat sat between them in front of the house.

But no sooner had she sat down than she jumped up again.
"I don't want people to think I do nothing but bake pies. I shall put one of my paintings in the picture as well."
"Simple pictures are best," warned the photographer.
But Ellen had already run off to fetch her painting.

When she returned, she leaned it against her chair.
The photographer threw his black cloth over the camera and crawled under it once more.

"We're ready," said the shoemaker and his wife. "What's wrong?"
"Smile," said the photographer.
"I can't," said Ellen.
"Neither can I," said the shoemaker.

So James ran into the garden and picked half a dozen turnips and ran back to the photographer and began to juggle with the turnips.
"Ha," said the shoemaker.
"Ho," said his wife.
But they did not smile.

Then James ran into the kitchen and fetched a giant frying pan and ran back to the photographer and stood on his head in the frying pan while juggling the turnips.

"Ha hum," said the shoemaker.

"Ho ha," said his wife.

But they did not smile.

Then James ran into the orchard and gathered a dozen apples. He did not see the bull browsing under the tree until the bull made a hideous noise. James dropped the apples and ran back to the photographer. The bull did not see James, but he *did* see the photographer.

"Ha, ha, ha!" laughed the shoemaker and his wife.

And James clicked the shutter.

Then the shoemaker and his wife jumped to their feet and caught the bull, tied him up, and helped the photographer to a chair.

"When will the picture be ready?" asked Ellen.
The photographer looked at his watch.
"Not long. It's developing right now."
In half a minute the photographer took out the film and opened it.
They all looked.

The photographer sighed. "Simple pictures are best."